Tizz

AT THE STAMPEDE

By Elisa Bialk

Pictures by Hildegard Lehmann

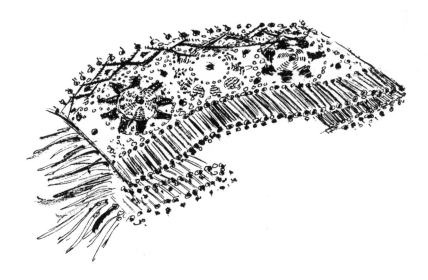

CHILDRENS PRESS, CHICAGO

This book is for

our godchild,

Laura Elisabeth Byron

Note:

I am especially indebted to D. C. Welden, Publicity Director for the Calgary Exhibition and Stampede, for helpful assistance in gathering background information for this book, and to his assistant, Miss Joan Plastow; and to Roland Bradley, Chairman of the Indian Committee for the exhibition, and his assistant, Ron Hall. I also wish to thank Michael Kartushyn, Indian Superintendent of the Blackfoot Reserve at Gleichen, Alberta, and Douglas Sobat, Office Manager at the Indian agency. My deepest gratitude goes to my longtime collaborator, chauffeur and mistake-catcher extraordinary, L. Martin Krautter — my husband.

Elisa Bialk

CONTENTS

"Ready?" Sheila Edmonds asked.

Tracy Hill said, *"Again?"*

Not that it wasn't fun, running around the track on this big ranch the Hills were visiting in the Canadian province of Alberta. But it would be even more fun to win sometimes, and Sheila had a horse that could run faster than Tracy's pony, Tizz.

Getting set in her saddle, Sheila coaxed, "Oh, come on! Be a sport."

Those words stung Tracy. Like her older brother Don, she wanted to be a good sport. Especially when she was a guest.

So she drew her palomino pony abreast of the thoroughbred gelding, Pepper. Sheila counted, "One, two, THREE!" and they were off.

Tizz was a good sport, too. She tried hard to keep up. Her beautiful cream-colored mane streamed back like a wave of wheat in the brisk breeze that swept off the plains. But her legs were shorter than Pepper's and she didn't have the same stride. Before they had circled the track for the first time, Tizz was falling behind.

Tracy thumped the pony with her heels, and Tizz made a brave try at catching up. Her neck darkened with sweat, and her sides heaved with the effort. Tracy knew Tizz was tired and felt sorry for the pony she loved so much. She simply couldn't force Tizz any more. Instead, she fell farther behind Sheila and the well-named Pepper.

Why hadn't she gone with Don and the others to see all of the ranch? Tracy asked herself. It was true she had chosen to stay behind, but how could she have known that Sheila had a horse that ran like the wind? After all, she hadn't met Sheila or any of the Edmonds family until yesterday. Their fathers knew each other through their cattle businesses. Mr. Edmonds had invited the Hills to come to Canada and be their guests at their ranch near Calgary, for the big Stampede.

Sheila pulled Pepper to a stop after she had run the agreed number of circles around the small track. The gelding did not seem at all winded when Tracy pulled up on Tizz, who was puffing and snorting and shaking her head sharply to show her displeasure.

"Your pony tires quickly, doesn't she?" Sheila commented.

Tracy was quick on the defense. "No, she doesn't. Back home in Arizona, Don and I ride in the desert every day, and Tizz keeps up with Don's horse very well."

Sheila's small sharp face took in the heaving sides, the snorting, and the sweat stains. "But look how she's panting."

"Running round and round in a circle trying to beat a horse must be harder than running *with* it," Tracy reasoned.

Her blue eyes lighted as they shifted to a rise in the distance. A line of horses was coming into view, which meant that the party was returning from its ride of inspection.

"Here they come!" Tracy shouted. "Let's go meet them." With blond ponytail bouncing, she rode Tizz toward the gate of the riding ring, glad for an excuse to leave.

Mr. and Mrs. Edmonds, Sheila's parents and hosts to the Hill family here in Alberta, were the first to greet the girls. He was a big man who carried his size with grace. She was tall and slender and quick in her movements, as well as in her manner of speaking and thinking.

Sheila's three older brothers were in the party.

9

Malcolm at sixteen seemed like a grown man to Tracy. Randy, twelve, was riding a horse as big and spirited as his father's. On the other hand Scott, who was fourteen, was drooping sidewise over his saddle as if he couldn't care less. All three boys were tall and slender like their mother, but they had bright red hair like their father. Of the four Edmonds children, only Sheila's hair was dark brown. Tracy thought this rather funny, as red hair would have suited Sheila just fine.

Naturally, the Hills looked so familiar to Tracy that they didn't need sorting out. She would certainly know ten-year-old Don anywhere, even if he weren't yelling and pretending he was going to lasso her with his saddle rope. If Tracy were a city block away, she could recognize her father's dark head, set nicely between broad shoulders. And there was her mother, her blond hair caught back in a ponytail like Tracy's, wearing jeans and a bright shirt and looking slim again, now that the new baby had come.

"Did you have fun, girls?" Mrs. Edmonds called when she rode up within earshot.

"Oh, yes," Tracy called back politely.

"We raced and raced," Sheila shouted, "but

Pepper beat Tizz every time."

Mrs. Edmonds' smile didn't change, but she spoke what Tracy was thinking: "My dear, one doesn't boast, you know."

She turned her smile on Tracy. "I'm sure Tizz runs very fast — for a pony."

Somehow, the kindly-meant words didn't make Tracy feel any better. As she patted Tizz's damp neck, she had the feeling that the comment didn't make Tizz happier, either. To Tracy, Tizz seemed like a human being who had the same feelings about everything that she had.

Later, in the guesthouse the Hills were occupying, Tracy asked her mother, "Is Sheila eight, or going on nine?"

"I believe her mother said she'd be nine in September."

Tracy nodded. Just as she thought. Sheila was more than a half-year older. But it wasn't only being older that made a difference. She admitted to her mother, "Sheila is not like the girls I know back home."

Mrs. Hill explained, as she combed the snarls out of Tracy's hair before bedtime, "Sheila has three older brothers. She's probably always tried to do whatever they do. That's why she's what might be called a tomboy."

"She certainly rides like a boy," Tracy agreed.

Don, overhearing the conversation, chimed in: "She rides better than Scott does, that's for sure, and he's older than I am."

Mr. Hill looked up from some papers he was going over. "Scott doesn't like to ride at all. He seems to have other interests."

Don made a funny sound. "Imagine a guy living on a ranch like this, with all these horses, and not liking to ride!"

"You'll probably run into a lot of people who are different from you," Mr. Hill said. "Getting to know them can be an interesting experience."

The hair-combing session over, Tracy put a jacket over her pajamas. "I'm going to say good night to Tizz," she called over her shoulder as she headed for the door.

No one thought this unusual, because at home she always did. But her mother cautioned, "Don't stay too long, dear. We'll have to be up early tomorrow. For the Stampede parade, you know."

Tracy climbed over the fence of the small corral in back of the guesthouse. She could have

opened the gate, but climbing over the fence was quicker.

Tizz was standing in a corner, looking for all the world as if she were thinking things over. Her pretty coloring was still clear, because although it was late in the evening, full darkness had not yet come. Days were very long, up north in July.

Tracy fondled her pony as she usually did, but the words she spoke were different. "Don't you worry, Tizz. You're as good as Pepper. Every bit as good!"

Tizz blinked her thick white lashes in surprise at the tone of Tracy's voice. She regarded her young owner with wide eyes, as if to say, "But of course—who said I wasn't?"

PART OF A DRAGON

Don had slept on a fold-up bed in the guest-house living room. Now, early the next morning, he awakened everyone by shouting from the big picture window, "Hey, everybody's up already, and getting the horses into the vans!"

His father, from the bedroom, said with a waking-up chuckle: "Well, this is one time it's not my responsibility!"

"What about Tizz?" Don wanted to know. They had brought the pony all the way from Arizona so that Tracy could ride her in the parade, and take part with her in a special exhibition at the Stampede.

"Transporting one pony to the fairgrounds won't be much of a job," his father said, coming into the living room for a better view. "Mr. Edmonds has promised to supply a whole string of his horses for the chuckwagon races and that's a big job."

"What are chuckwagon races?"

"You'll find out in good time." Mr. Hill squinted through the window to see better. "We'd better get out and give them a hand."

15

Tracy reached for her clothes sleepily. "Doesn't it ever get dark here?" she wondered. Although it was early, it was bright daylight and the sun was shining.

"Don't forget to stop for breakfast at the big house," Mrs. Hill called as Don and his father hurried out. "It will be a big day."

"You know what?" Don commented as he and his father walked over to where the horses were being loaded. "I saw Scott go out carrying a guitar and cords and all kinds of gear, and get into a car with some people and drive away. Guess that means he's not coming to the parade."

"Maybe everybody in and around Calgary isn't going to the parade," his father suggested.

"Boy, I wouldn't miss it for anything! Not from what I've heard about it."

In spite of all Don had heard, neither he nor Tracy was prepared for the crowds already lining the streets when they pulled into Calgary. Nor were they prepared for Calgary itself, a big modern city, with a view of the high peaks of the Canadian Rockies in the distance.

Thousands of people were jamming the streets and sidewalks. Some had brought portable camp stoves on which they were cooking pancakes for themselves and friends. Other early-birds had brought lunches which they were eating as if they were at a picnic in the park, while waiting for the parade to begin.

As could be expected, there was a great deal of confusion. There were bands, floats, tribes of fancily-dressed Indians on horses decked out in beading, colorful Royal Canadian Mounted Police, groups of singing school children, and large sections of residents of Calgary and nearby towns who were representing all sorts of clubs.

But Mr. Edmonds had been through all of this before. Somehow, he got his party to the starting place in time, and led a group of riders mounted on his beautiful horses. Except Tracy of course, who rode Tizz. Sheila rode next to her on Pepper, and Don paired off with Randy.

A photographer jumped in front of Tracy and Sheila and took a picture, then asked Tracy her name and where she was from. When she said, "Tucson, Arizona," he told her: "That's a long way to come—but there's an Indian band from Arizona in the parade, too."

Then he called to Sheila, "And what's your

name, Sonny-Boy?"

"Sonny-Boy!" Sheila hooted. "I'm a girl and my name's Sheila Edmonds."

The photographer grinned. "Righto! I don't have to ask where you're from. I know your father."

When he was gone Tracy said, "I guess he thought you were a boy on account of your short hair." She was trying to be nice in case Sheila's feelings had been hurt, but the Canadian girl only shrugged and said, "I wouldn't be bothered with long hair for anything."

Riding in the parade was exciting, but Tracy wished she could see the Indian band from Arizona,

and other paraders she was missing. She caught
just a glimpse of a wagon drawn by a team of
buffalo, and longed to see the animals close up.

Don was feeling the same way. Excitement
was stirring him up so much that it was hard for
him to hold his horse in, as he had to do to keep
step with the other paraders. When he passed a
side street where another group was waiting to
join in, he could hardly believe his eyes. Waiting
there was something that looked like a great
Chinese dragon.

"What was *that?*" he yelled to Randy.

"The Chinese section," Randy yelled back over the noise. "They use that dragon only on their New Year's, and for the Stampede parade."

Don looked back, stretching his neck for another view, but the surge of the crowd closed it off.

Randy waved to a friend on the sidewalk who was calling to him, and had an idea. "Say," he said to Don, "if you'd like to watch the parade awhile, there's a friend of mine who'll be glad to ride your horse."

"Okay!" Don decided on the spur of the moment. It took only seconds to make the switch.

"Meet you at the main gate of the fairgrounds when the parade breaks up," Randy shouted as he rode on with his new partner.

Don made his way along the curb to where he had seen the great Chinese dragon. It was entering the mainstream of the parade, a giant serpent weaving this way and that. There were Chinese boys and men running alongside it.

Sometimes Don's father joked that his middle name was Curiosity. It certainly seemed to be true now. Don couldn't keep from running alongside the great dragon himself.

Nor could he keep from peeking underneath a part of the weaving column. A bright Chinese face met his curious glance with a grin.

"Want to take a turn?" the boy offered.

"Sure!"

He slipped under the dragon, and the Chinese boy slipped out, and ran at his side. All Don could see of him were his feet, but he knew he was there.

"It's heavier than it looks," the Chinese boy called, telling Don something he had found out for himself. "When you get tired, I will take your place."

Running while holding up his part of the dragon was tiring, Don had to admit. But it was such fun he hated to give up his place.

Presently the boy belonging to the feet running beside him popped under the dragon, next to him. "Maybe there is room for both of us," he grinned. "Boys do not take up as much room as men. But only men can carry the head. It weighs over fifty pounds."

After a while, still another boy popped under the dragon in their place. When his new friend stepped out, Don felt it was time that he did, too.

"Thanks," Don said when they were in sunlight once more. Politely, he added, "My name's Don Hill and I'm from Tucson, Arizona."

"My name is Harry Ling and I am from Calgary, by way of China," the boy said with his wide smile. He was fishing in his pocket as he spoke. Bringing out a small, rather battered card, he handed it to Don with an invitation. "Come and see us." Then he ran after the dragon.

Don looked at the card. It bore the name of a Chinese restaurant. He tucked it into the pocket of his shirt with the thought that, while in Calgary, he would like to visit it.

Then, edging through the throngs, he began working his way towards the fairgrounds. Even a two-hour parade finally comes to an end, and he didn't want to miss Randy, or any of the fun and excitement that still lay ahead.

Tracy knew what she was to do after the parade. The plan had been worked out before the Hills came to Alberta. She and Tizz — and Sheila and Pepper — were going over to an exhibition called Flare Square, which showed the history of Canada. Included in it was a copy of an old homestead, with a corral, and there the foursome would play at being pioneers. Mrs. Edmonds was a member of the society sponsoring the exhibit. She had agreed to be on duty every day, so she and the girls could come and go together.

After the parade, the hungry Hills and Edmonds' had lunch together before scattering for the afternoon. Only Scott was not with them. His mother told the Hills that his band was working so much all through the Stampede that he'd have very little free time, if any.

Mr. Edmonds announced that he and Mr. Hill were going over to the auction at the stockyards after lunch. "Want to come along, Malcolm?" he asked his oldest son.

"Thanks, Dad, but if you don't mind, I'd like to go over to the Exhibition office and see who's checking in for the rodeo."

Randy spoke up eagerly. "I ought to go there too, and sign up for the steer-riding event."

Mrs. Hill's eyes widened. "Can boys Randy's age ride steers, in Canada?"

Mr. Edmonds nodded. "We have a special event for boys under fourteen. There are two schools of thought about it," he admitted. "Some feel they're too young, others that it's the only way they can get early training. I try to let the boys decide for themselves, when they're ready."

"Personally, I think twelve is a bit young," Mrs. Edmonds put in, "but I told Randy that if he had his heart set on it, I wouldn't interfere."

"I'd like to ride a steer, myself!" Don declared.

"Better wait till you've ridden a few in practice," Malcolm advised in a big-brother fashion. "It's not easy."

Mrs. Edmonds looked at her watch. "I'm due at Flare Square right now." Her eyes swept the group finishing lunch. "Why don't those of you who are free come along for a quick look-see?"

Within minutes, all except the two fathers and Malcolm were inside the exhibit, which traced the history of Canada from an early Hudson's Bay

Company trading post at one end, to space-age marvels at the other. The high tower, from the top of which a flame of natural gas burned, was a landmark which could be seen for miles around.

Don and Randy had their attention caught by a reproduction of an old "assay office." It was to a place such as this that the miners had brought their gold to be weighed, during gold-rush days.

Mrs. Edmonds led Mrs. Hill and the girls to a sod hut, explaining, "We've tried to be as careful

as possible with the copies we've made here. You'd be surprised if you knew how long it took our group to find that spinning wheel in there, and that butter churn, and that old cradle. The bunk beds could be copied, and so could those furs which were used as blankets. Even so, somebody had to check everything down to the last detail so that it would be exactly the way it was."

"Were there many sod huts like this, used by farmers?" Mrs. Hill asked.

"Yes, farming gradually replaced buffalo hunting and gold mining. You see, after the railway was built in 1883, many settlers came from everywhere."

Tracy was listening with interest, but the boys had wandered off on their own exploration. Now Don called, "Hey, look at me!" There he was at an old shanty called the "Rustler's Roost," his face thrust through a hole in a sign marked, "Wanted — Dead or Alive — for Rustling at the Calgary Stampede."

Next to a chuckwagon with bins marked for the supplies it had carried, was the pioneer cabin where Tracy and Sheila were to be a live attraction. Tizz and Pepper were already at home in the corral next to it. Although she and her pony had been separated only a short time, Tracy climbed the corral fence as eagerly as if she hadn't seen Tizz for ages.

Mrs. Edmonds was anxious to get back to the entrance to Flare Square, where she was needed to answer the many questions asked by people crowding into the exhibit. She handed the girls their costumes, and Mrs. Hill stayed to help them into the wraparound calico long-skirted dresses, with matching sunbonnets.

Even Sheila looked girlish in hers, but she complained, "I'm boiling!"

Tracy didn't mind. This might seem like a hot day to people who lived in Alberta, but it would have been considered cool in Arizona.

There was a door in the back of the "old homestead" which led directly into the main street. The girls had been told they could exercise Tizz and Pepper before the exhibition opened to the public, and when the crowds were thin. Right now it appeared as if the crowds would never thin. Tracy kept busy combing Tizz's mane with the comb she had brought along, so that she wouldn't notice all the people looking at them.

Entertainment was going on in the center of a grandstand on the exhibit grounds. The girls had been invited to take turns and go over to hear the bands play, or to see the folk dances, whenever they got bored. Sheila went more often than Tracy, who soon got used to being stared at. When she heard people say, "What a cute pony!" she didn't mind a bit.

What she did mind, though, was going home when night came and leaving her pony behind. Mr. Edmonds had decided that Tizz and Pepper couldn't be transported back and forth every day, and had to stay on the fairgrounds with the rest of the horses. Tracy was used to saying good night to Tizz before going to bed, and hated to think of her being miles away.

Sheila noticed with what sadness Tracy said good-bye when it was time to go. "You spoil that pony!" she said.

"I don't spoil her," Tracy denied quickly. "I just don't want her to get lonesome."

Sheila said with a grin, "She won't get lonesome."

When they were all riding back to the ranch in the station wagon, Don said to his parents,

"Randy wants me to share his room instead of sleeping in the guesthouse. Okay?"

"That's fine with us," Mr. Hill agreed.

"We could use another boy around the house," Mr. Edmonds said with a laugh. "Scott's so busy with his band during the Stampede, we hardly get to see him."

As they were getting out at the ranch, Sheila said, rather shyly for Sheila, "Tracy, I've got an extra bed in my room, too, if you'd like to share it."

"Thank you," Tracy answered politely, "but — I like the guesthouse."

When her mother was saying good night, she added thoughtfully, "Tracy, perhaps you should have accepted Sheila's invitation. She's an only girl in a family of boys, you know. She might want very much to share her room with another girl when she has a chance."

"Sheila!" Tracy echoed. She couldn't imagine a tomboy like Sheila Edmonds wanting to share anything with anyone.

"Good night, Mother." Tracy's words slurred into weariness. She had had a big day. Whether Tizz was close to her or not, in a moment she was asleep.

TALK ABOUT EXCITEMENT!

Tracy didn't complain about getting up early the next morning. She could hardly wait to get to the fairgrounds and Tizz.

As she dressed, it seemed strangely quiet without Don around being noisy, as ten-year-old boys can be. The thought passed through her head that it must have been fun, sleeping in the big house. Yet Tracy still thought she'd prefer to share the guesthouse with her parents. She still didn't feel quite at home with Sheila. Besides, since her baby brother had come, she hadn't had much chance to be alone with her mother and father.

This was the afternoon they were going to the Stampede, and driving to Calgary in the station wagon, Don and Randy and Sheila talked about nothing else. Tracy noticed that Sheila never said a word about Pepper. This seemed strange to her. She was sure the Stampede would be fun, but after all, it was a rodeo and she already had seen several. To her, it couldn't compare with being with a pet of one's own, particularly when that pet meant as much to her as Tizz did.

At Flare Square, Mrs. Edmonds suggested that Don and Randy walk along with the girls while they exercised Tizz and Pepper before the crowds started coming. In her independent way, Sheila protested that she knew her way around well enough to go alone.

"Perhaps you do," Mrs. Edmonds smiled, "but it's always nice for a girl to have an escort, anyhow."

So the boys tagged along. The fairgrounds had not yet opened to the public, but there was much excitement. Horses were being ridden from the corrals to areas where they would be needed. Cattle and sheep were being moved into the livestock barns. Don, who had come to know something about sheep when he had made friends with a 4-H boy at a stock show in Texas, saw a variety that was new to him. These were white sheep with black heads and white markings. Randy said they were an English variety called Suffolk.

Randy also pointed out a big exhibition building which, he said, led a double life. In the winter it was a curling house. Curling, he said, was the most popular family sport in Canada.

Tizz and Pepper not only had to sidestep cattle and sheep, but "litter-pillars" as well. These were motorized units joined together in sections and painted a bright green, with the word "litter-pillar" lettered on the side. They moved and looked like huge caterpillars. Crews on the litter-pillars emptied waste containers and picked up all the litter that was bound to be strewn along the ground when so many thousands of people came to a fair.

Two Indian boys came trotting along, bareback, leading a string of horses. Randy called, "Hi, Leonard," to one of them, who waved in answer.

"They're taking the horses to the Indian Village," Randy observed. "Let's follow them."

Smoke was rising from many of the tepees that were spread out in a great circle in an enclosure. Signs identified the tribes as Blackfoot, Stoney, Sarcee and Peigan.

The Indian boys and horses disappeared behind some tepees. Randy turned back in the direction from which they had come, explaining, "It's more fun to be in the village when the Indians are doing their tribal dances, or when their tepees are open for inspection."

They went back to Flare Square in time for Tracy and Sheila to play pioneers at the old homestead. Often during the morning, Sheila said, "I can't wait till we go to the Stampede!" Tracy didn't complain, because she was with Tizz.

Once at the Stampede, though, Tracy found herself wrapped up in one of the most exciting afternoons of her life. Being out-of-doors on a bright sunny day in a big stadium, watching one event after another in a packed program, was fun in itself. And what events they were, besides the breathtaking ones she had come to know, like bronco busting and Brahma bull riding! There

were also special ones that were new not only to her, but to all of the Hills.

For instance, there was a wild cow milking contest which was just as wild as it sounded. The cows — off the range, not off farms — were let loose in the infield arena. At a given signal, the cowboys who were entered dashed into the herd on horseback and lassoed a cow. After each dismounted and tied his cow, his helper joined him on foot. It was the helper's job to milk the cow, using a small bottle for the milk.

Malcolm was one of the helpers, so naturally,

all the Edmonds' and the Hills rooted for his team. That is, when they could stop laughing. It was a funny sight, watching the mad scrambling in the infield, with the cows mooing loudly and trying to run away, and the cowboys, helpers and horses all jumbled together. Malcolm's cow wouldn't stand still long enough to be milked, and before he really got going, someone else ran to the judges' stand with the required milk supply.

"He might have better luck tomorrow," Mr. Edmonds said, wiping his eyes which were wet from laughing.

Malcolm also took part in the wild horse event, which was another new one to the Hills. Mr. Edmonds explained that most of the amateurs turned out for these unusual events because it gave them a chance to earn some money without competing with the top rodeo pros, who were entered in the regular events.

In the wild horse event, a team of three had to hold and saddle a horse as it came through the gate, and one of the team had to ride it across the arena to the pickup chutes. This time Malcolm's job was to hold the horse at the end of the rope attached to its halter. It was easy to see those horses were really wild. Mr. Edmonds said some ranchers, including Indians, made their living by raising wild horses for rodeos.

But what really stirred Don to fever pitch was the boys' wild steer riding contest. Although the steers and young heifers used were chosen and graded with special care, the kids came bucking out of the chutes just like the adult competitors. Don watched with special interest as a young Indian boy stayed on for the required number of seconds, and chalked up extra points by moving his feet back and forth in the regulation manner.

Don thought he recognized the boy. He asked Randy, "Isn't that the kid we saw bringing in the horses to the Indian Village this morning?"

"Yes, that's Leonard Foxchief. He's good. Most of the Indian kids are," Randy added. "They ride a lot more than we do."

Don spoke his thought out loud. "I'd like to ride a steer."

The thought of it held his imagination until the intermission showtime. Then acts came on such as he and Tracy had never seen before. Trained Brahma bulls were put through their paces as if they were small dogs. A beautiful white and an equally beautiful black stallion showed how they put on pretend-battles for the movies. And there was a Rocket Man who was projected from the ground of the arena high into the air, and then down right onto the center of the stage.

When the show was over, everyone felt keyed up and hungry. Mr. Edmonds spoke of a good restaurant that might be interesting. Mrs. Edmonds said she'd have to be excused from joining the party, as she had promised to be on duty at Flare Square that night.

Mention of Flare Square brought immediate thoughts of Tizz to Tracy. Had she been lonesome this afternoon? Was she nervous, with all those strangers staring at her, and no Tracy around?

She spoke up before the group separated. "I'd like to go with you, Mrs. Edmonds."

She did. The two stopped at an outdoor food stand for fish and chips and corn-on-the-cob served on a stick. Then together, they went to Flare Square, where the tower of flame was really striking now that evening had come. But Tracy scarcely saw the spectacle. A small pony fitted her vision better than the sky-high flare.

PANCAKES ON HORSEBACK

Mr. Edmonds had a surprise for the Hills. He kept it to himself until they were all riding back to the ranch in the station wagon together. Then he announced that the Hills, as visitors from the United States, had been invited to ride in the Blackfoot Indian parade that would take place in the morning. Six wagons and carriages dating back to the gold-rush days would lead the parade. Places for Mr. and Mrs. Hill were being held in one of them. Tracy and Don could ride alongside the wagon.

"What fun!" Mrs. Hill exclaimed.

Tracy asked, "May I ride Tizz?"

"Sure thing!" Mr. Edmonds assured her. "That's what she's here for. And Don can ride the same horse he rode in the opening parade."

The next morning, the Edmonds family decided to go along with the Hills before going on to the fairgrounds. The parade was to begin at the Palliser Hotel where, it turned out, Scott's band would be playing at that time.

"It's about the only chance we'll get to see him perform," Mrs. Edmonds explained. "We never seem to be near a TV set when he's on."

Don was impressed. "Does Scott play on TV?" he asked.

"Oh, yes. His group is quite well known in Calgary." To Mrs. Hill, she added, "We mothers take turns chauffeuring because they're all too young to drive. I'm off the hook this week because of my Flare Square job, but I'll make it up later."

"I'll say you will," Randy agreed. "I'll tell you one thing, though—I wouldn't want to miss all the fun Scott's missing this week, for all the money in the world."

"Scott doesn't do it only for money, Randy," his father corrected. "He happens to find playing in the band more fun than anything else."

When Don saw Scott in action the next morning at the hotel, he began to understand what music meant to him. There he was on a platform with three other young musicians and a girl singer. They were surprisingly good. If Don didn't know this was a young people's band playing country-western, he'd never guess it by the sound. It couldn't be easy to get up early and stay up late and miss all the action at the Stampede. It just *had* to be that Scott enjoyed playing in a band more than riding a steer as Randy intended doing, or taking part in all the events he could sign up for, like Malcolm.

As they were listening to the band, the Hills were told that the White Horse & Yukon Pass stage in which they were to ride was ready and waiting. Mr. and Mrs. Hill were sharing it with a family from Montreal, who had won the trip as a prize.

Don noticed that a boy about his age was in the party. As he rode alongside the wagon on his horse, he tried to strike up a conversation, but the boy merely smiled and didn't answer. His mother spoke for him, in careful, halting English: "My son speaks only French."

Well, he learned something new each day! Don thought. He had noticed that many of the signs in Canada were printed in English and in French. What he had not realized was that in some areas in Canada, only French was spoken.

On the other side of the wagon, Tracy was learning something else. A man came up to her with a big platter of pancakes, each wrapped around a sausage, and asked her to help herself.

"What about your pony?" he joked.

"I think Tizz would rather have a carrot."

"We're fresh out of carrots, but have another pancake for yourself, then."

Tracy did. They were awfully good. It seemed to her that she had never tasted better ones. For that matter, she had never eaten pancakes on horseback, before. It was a pleasant custom. During the Stampede, the restaurants on the route of a parade cooked and served pancakes to the paraders.

There was another pleasant Stampede custom in Calgary. Stores and business groups held giant free barbecues and what were called "sidewalk breakfasts." One such breakfast was in progress now along the route of the parade. Hundreds of people lined one intersection, eating beans and bacon and bread served by a big department store that had set up counters right outside its doors. The informal diners held their paper plates with one hand and waved with the other. Tracy waved back.

When the parade stopped for a few minutes because of a traffic jam, Tracy looked back. She cried, "Oh, how pretty!" as she saw a young foal running alongside a mare in the Blackfoot Indian section, without even a lead rope to guide it.

Don heard her exclamation and looked back, too. "Let's ride over for a closer look," he suggested. Together, they did.

The foal was about the same size as Tizz, and almost the same color. The mare was decorated in beautiful beading, the same kind which decorated the costume of the Indian girl riding it.

Tracy hoped Tizz and the foal could get acquainted, but the mare got a little skittish as the strangers drew near. Besides, the parade was starting up again, and she and Don ought to be back escorting the wagon.

The Indian girl smiled in friendly under-standing as the children turned back. "Come and see us at the Indian Village after the parade," she invited.

When the parade and the Indian ceremonies were over, the Hills decided to accept the invitation. The girl who had ridden the mare recognized the children as they approached the big semicircle of tepees. "Welcome to our village!" she said in her friendly way. "Our tepee is open for inspection,

if you would like to see it."

They followed her into it through the flap that served as entrance. Light came from the top of the tepee, where there was an opening like a skylight. On the floor was a circle of furs and blankets, which served as beds. In the center of the circle was a cookstove with a pot in which something good was cooking. Hanging from the sides of the tepee were more samples of the beautiful bead-work the girl and the man had worn in the parade.

"My grandmother made all of it," the girl said proudly as the Hills admired it. "She's teaching us, too," she added with a modest smile, "but we are not so good yet."

"So many of you seem to have artistic talent," Mrs. Hill said, warming to the girl's friendliness. "I do a little painting myself, and I've been impressed with the fine artwork on exhibit in the Big Four building."

"Did you see the head of a young girl which won a prize? That was mine."

"Yes, I remember it very well. You plan to go on with your artwork, I hope?"

"If I have time," the girl answered. "In the fall, I go to college."

Don slipped out of the tepee while his mother and the girl were chatting. It was interesting but hot in that tepee. Outside, the first person he saw was the Indian boy who had ridden the steer in the rodeo yesterday.

"Hey, you're Leonard Foxchief!" Don called. "I saw you ride that steer yesterday."

A smile softened Leonard's tan face. "I'll ride again today. Will you be there?"

"Guess not. We don't have tickets."

Leonard took a small white slip out of his pocket. "Everybody who rides gets a free pass," he said, handing the slip to Don. "You may have this, but you'll have to sit in the infield bleachers."

"Thanks, that's just where I want to sit!"

The rest of the Hills came out of the tepee. Tracy was anxious to get back to Flare Square and the corral that was Tizz's home away from home. Her parents walked her back to it, and Don went off to the grandstand enclosure with his new friend Leonard Foxchief.

CHUCKWAGON RACES

Watching the rodeo from a fence in the infield seemed to Don the most exciting thing he had ever done. Sometimes the cowboys riding the broncs and the steers and the Brahma bulls came so close that those sitting on the fence had to jump quickly to the other side.

When it was time for Leonard Foxchief to leave for the boys' steer-riding event, Don was joined by Randy Edmonds, who climbed up saying, "Your Dad told me you were here."

"How'd you get in?"

"The man at the gate lets me in because Dad's an exhibitor. Mother thought you'd rather sit in the grandstand, where you can see more."

See more? Mothers were funny people! Down here in the infield bleachers, Don not only saw everything that was going on, he could get the hot smell of the dust and the animals. It was the next best thing to riding himself.

When the boys' steer-riding event was announced, Don asked Randy, "When do you ride?"

"Day after tomorrow. I was late signing up, so I've got to wait my turn."

Don spoke up boldly. "Do you suppose there's a chance I could get to ride a steer?"

Randy looked uncertain. "I hardly think so."

Someone else crowded next to them on the fence. There wasn't much room, but the third person didn't need much. It was skinny Sheila. The three rooted for Leonard Foxchief when he came bouncing out on his steer. His time was the best of all the boys riding, which meant he won a cash prize.

Exciting as the afternoon had been, more was in store when the Edmonds' and the Hills sat in the grandstand for the evening show, which would begin with the chuckwagon races.

"It's too bad Scott can't be with us," Mrs. Edmonds said, "but his band is playing tonight."

From the tone of her voice, Tracy knew Mrs. Edmonds missed her son. She in turn missed Tizz. She wished she could be down there in the infield on Tizz, the way the queen of the Stampede and her assistants were mounted on horses and standing at attention with the grand marshal.

"Where's Malcolm?" Don asked Randy.

"He's going to be an outrider tonight."

"What's an outrider?"

"You'll see," Randy grinned. "It's easier to see than to explain."

"Wait till you see those chuckwagon races!" Sheila was saying to Tracy. The words came out rather slurred, because her teeth were sticking into the taffy apple she was eating.

Tracy smiled politely, trying to hide the fact that she was a bit peeved at Sheila. That afternoon when the tomboy had learned Randy and Don were at the rodeo, she couldn't bear to stay in the corral at Flare Square. Asking Tracy to keep an eye on Pepper, she had slipped out of her costume and out of the rear door of the old homestead on the exhibition grounds, and hadn't come back for a couple of hours. Tracy had found that it was much less fun to be in the corral alone than with a friend, even when the friend was as different as Sheila.

However, now the chuckwagon races were about to begin, and in a moment everything else was forgotten. None of the Hills had seen an event like it before.

Each wagon had a crew of five men, the driver and four outriders. The wagons were pulled by four of the same kind of fast thoroughbreds that the outriders used, so there was plenty of action.

But there were rules that made it more than just a race. At a given signal, the drivers brought the wagons into the infield, where the outriders were waiting on foot. At another signal, the outriders had to toss tent poles and a camp stove into the wagon.

Only then could the driver start. Before going out on the track, though, he had to complete a figure eight around barrel markers. This was done so quickly that often two or three wagons hit the track at the same time, and began to race neck and neck.

Meanwhile, after the wagons were loaded, the outriders leaped onto their horses. They too had to complete a figure eight around those barrels before they could take off after their wagon.

The wagons went so fast that the outriders had a hard time catching up. The people watching could easily connect the outriders with their wagon because they and the driver wore the same-colored jackets. Points were won if the outriders finished with the driver, and lost if they did not. Points were also lost if any of the barrel markers were knocked over, or if there was some kind of accident

that might hold back any of the other riders, such as a camp stove falling out of a wagon.

There were ten chuckwagon races, and each seemed faster than the one before. When Malcolm's turn came as an outrider, he had trouble getting his horse to do the figure eight around the barrels, and got a late start. He rode with his feet high in the stirrups, his back bent low over his mount's neck like a jockey. Even so, he couldn't catch up until the race was over.

Mr. Edmonds shook his head. "Tough luck. It's not easy to get a horse to do a figure eight around those barrels, and this is only Malcolm's first year as an outrider."

"But he's practiced and practiced," Randy said in disappointment.

"It's mighty different when you do it around some barrels set up on your own ranch, and down there with all the confusion going on." Mr. Edmonds smiled as he promised his younger son, "You'll see."

In spite of Malcolm falling behind, his outfit didn't do badly in points. An outrider with another wagon had knocked over a barrel, and one driver had to slow down when a wheel on his wagon loosened. The wagons used in the races were especially built and lighter than the real ones had been. Even Tracy could tell that, as she saw the old-fashioned one next to the old homestead at Flare Square every day.

Her parents were as excited as she and Don were. "I've never seen anything like it in all my life!" Mr. Hill declared. "This must have been what chariot races were like."

"They're pretty fast," Mr. Edmonds agreed. "Tonight's races won't set any records, either. There'll be faster ones."

Yet it seemed as if the ten races had been run in almost no time at all. They were followed by a program of very good entertainment.

But for Don and Tracy, the show had ended with the chuckwagon races. Don's mind stayed with them, running them over and over. Sometimes he pictured himself as the driver of the wagon, hunched forward in the teetering seat, practically flying around the track. Sometimes he was an outrider like Malcolm, doing his job in loading the wagon, then leaping onto his horse and taking after the wagon in a whirl of dust.

As for Tracy, her mind wandered, too. She

couldn't quite picture Tizz harnessed with three horses to a chuckwagon, but she could picture herself on Tizz as an outrider, racing like the wind after the wagon. And of course, in her mind's eye, Tizz never fell behind. Never.

It had been a full day, and the show was a long one. Tracy leaned against her mother, meaning to close her eyes for just a minute. The next thing she knew, her mother was shaking her gently and saying, "The show is over, Tracy. Time to go home."

"We mustn't forget Tizz," she said sleepily.

"You must have been dreaming, dear. Tizz has been bedded down for the night long ago. You'll see her again in the morning."

Somehow, morning did not seem too far away. Here in Alberta, it had a way of coming quickly.

DAY OFF?

It came about when Mrs. Edmonds realized as they all sat around the big breakfast table in the ranch kitchen: "Goodness, here you are in Calgary for the first time, and you're not seeing anything but the fairgrounds!"

Don answered, "What's so bad about that?"

"I love the fairgrounds. So does Tizz." That, of course, was Tracy speaking.

Mrs. Hill protested, "I haven't seen all the exhibits, yet."

Mr. Hill pointed out, "I've been giving so much of my time to business, I'm 'way behind the rest of you."

But Mrs. Edmonds had a strong will. "You can't go back to Arizona without seeing something of Calgary. We're proud of our city. The country-side is lovely, too, with those mountain peaks looming in the west."

"Next week," Don remembered, "we'll be in the Canadian Rockies."

"But this week," Mrs. Edmonds said, "you should see what's east of them. You all need a day off."

"Who'll take care of Tizz?" Tracy asked.

"I will," Sheila offered promptly. "It'll be fun to exercise her. Why, I've never ridden a pony!" Her button-bright eyes crinkled as she grinned widely. "Besides, I owe you sitter's service."

"What do you mean?" Mrs. Edmonds asked.

Sheila tossed her short-cropped head. "Yesterday I sneaked out the back way and went over to the rodeo. Tracy had to take care of both Tizz and Pepper."

"You might have told me, Sheila. You didn't have to sneak."

"It was more fun that way. And I thought Tracy would tell you."

She flashed a look at Tracy which said plainly, I-thought-you-would-but-I'm-glad-you-didn't. For the first time, Tracy felt the warmth of friendship behind that tough little tomboy hide. Her heart lost its sinking feeling. She could trust Sheila to take good care of Tizz.

Armed with a list of places to see, the Hills set out. They went to interesting spots in the city, and then headed for Heritage Park. It was set in rolling countryside with a good view of those beautiful Canadian Rockies they would visit soon.

The park, they had been told, was kept up by the historical society to which Mrs. Edmonds belonged. She had promised them that it was considerably bigger than Flare Square, and it was. There was a railroad train which carried visitors from the entrance to the rebuilt village street.

The train seemed different because, instead of short seats running crosswise with an aisle in the middle, it had seats that ran the whole length of the coaches. The conductor explained that the long seats had been installed during the old days when the railroad was being built. Workers had been transported back and forth by train each day to where the tracks were being laid, and more workmen could be fitted into the cars with those long seats.

The Hills got off the train in the "village" and went through the houses and shops, rebuilt exactly as they had once been. The old hotel, with its dining room bigger than the lobby, could have come right out of a TV western. Don half-expected a sheriff to come charging in with a couple of six-shooters, looking for the town badman. Any bandit, though, would have a hard time getting away, because just up the street was the office of

the "Mounties." (The Canadian police are still called "Mounties", although most of the men ride in patrol cars now.) "You know what their motto is?" Don asked Tracy. *"Maintain the Right."*

In an oldtime blacksmith shop, a smith showed how he shoed horses and forged ironwork. Back of the shop was a copy of the first electric plant installed. Two instruction sheets were pasted on the wall, one in English and one in Chinese. Mr. Hill answered the children's puzzled expression by explaining that there had been a lot of Chinese laborers in Canada in pioneer days. They had come to work on the railroad, and many of them had stayed on. With their families they were among the oldest settlers.

Mrs. Hill called their attention to an old dentist's office, showing horrid-looking drills and tools. The dentist's chair had been a folding one, so that he could pack it into his wagon and take it from one town to another on his route. "Remember this office when you complain about going to your modern dentist back home," she suggested jokingly.

There was so much to see, it was dinnertime before the family realized how late it was. Don had a sudden thought. "Say, as long as we're not on the fairgrounds today, why don't we eat at that restaurant the Chinese boy told me about?"

"A good idea," his father agreed.

After some digging, Don brought out the card the boy had given him, now very much the worse for wear. The Hills headed for Calgary's Chinatown. There were markets with barbecued ducks and strings of black mushrooms and other mysterious foods they couldn't identify hanging in the windows. Some of the restaurants were shaped like pagodas.

The restaurant which Harry Ling's family owned was on the second floor, and it was crowded with the Chinese people who lived in the area. This was fine with the Hills, as it gave them a chance to sample real Chinese food. It was different but delicious. Even Tracy, who could be quite picky, enjoyed it.

Harry came out of the kitchen and over to the Hills' table, grinning the same kind of big grin Don had first seen under the dragon during the opening Stampede parade. "Ah, I see you have come!" He shook hands with Don and bowed to the other members of the family.

"Do you work here all the time?" Don asked.

"Only after school," Harry said. "This place is run by my family, so —." He shrugged. "We Chinese families all work together."

"So do we," Don said quickly. Of course, he didn't help with the cooking, but he thought it best not to mention that.

After Harry had to go back to the kitchen and the big meal they had ordered was finished, Mr. Hill asked, "Well, what now?"

Don spoke up. "If you ask me — let's go to the fairgrounds. We haven't been to the Midway yet."

"Yes, let's!" Tracy joined in. In the back of her mind was the thought that if they went to the fairgrounds, she might get to see Tizz.

So, "day off" or not, the Hills ended up at the fairgrounds after all. Going on some of the rides was great fun, and to Tracy being on the Ferris wheel with her father when it stopped at the highest point was scary but exciting.

Then she saw a merry-go-round that had real ponies for small children to ride. She got so lonesome that she made the family walk to the corral where Tizz was spending the night.

"Is this supposed to be a day off?" Mr. Hill

complained good-naturedly as he led his family to Tizz's "home away from home." The walk in itself was fun, though. The children could see all the bright lights of the Midway. As they passed the Indian Village they stopped to see the dancing that was going on, on a platform built around a big tree.

It was hard to tell who looked sleepier when they got together, Tracy or Tizz. Tracy hugged her pony and asked, "Did you miss me?"

She was holding Tizz so tightly that the pony shook her head up and down, to free it. Of course to Tracy, Tizz was plainly saying, "Yes."

AT THE BLACKFOOT RESERVE

Don heard some news the next day that upset him. Leonard Foxchief had been thrown by a steer and injured.

He thought of Leonard as a friend, and so he set out to go to the Indian Village and ask about him. Getting there was easy enough. Finding the right tepee was another matter. The village looked different than it had when he had visited it before, either when tepees were open for inspection or when tribal dances were going on.

This morning only Indians were about, some visiting friends camped here for the Stampede. Remembering his Cub Scout Indian lore, Don was reminded of the summer roundups when various tribes used to get together. A big difference was that instead of having to hunt for meat and roots for food as they used to, the heads of families merely went to the office in the village to pick up rations provided by the Canadian government.

Don recalled that the tepee used by the Foxchief family was painted pink and decorated with animals, but there were several that answered that description. There was also an oddly streaked reddish-pink one, which had been painted the night before a rainstorm by an Indian who had never gotten around to repainting it a solid color. *That* one, Don was sure, did not belong to the Foxchiefs!

As he wandered about, he saw the girl he and his family had talked to after the Indian parade. She was easy to remember because, while she wore the required native costume, she also wore glasses with modern frames.

The girl recognized him, too, and greeted him warmly. Don noticed that she talked carefully, as if she were translating from another language. Actually, this is what a lot of the young Indians did. Leonard had told him that many spoke only Indian dialect at home, until they went to school.

Don got to the point at once. "I heard that Leonard was hurt yesterday, and I came to find out how he's doing."

"He was not hurt bad, but he cannot ride the rest of the week. So he went back to the reserve with Grandfather."

"Could I go out and see him there?"

"If you can find the house." She gave him instructions for getting to the reserve that sounded easy.

Don thanked her, and went to look for his father. He found him with Mr. Edmonds in one of the livestock buildings. They were inspecting the handsome white breed of cattle he knew was called *Shar-Lay*. He could say it, but he thought he probably never would be able to spell it— *Charolais*.

Don's father decided he'd like to see an Indian reserve himself, but Mr. Edmonds had promised to be a judge in a cattle event due to begin, and couldn't join them.

"Let's see if your mother and sister want to come along," Mr. Hill suggested.

They stopped at Flare Square, and were surprised to find Mrs. Hill stationed at the entrance gate, answering questions like a native Calgarian. She explained that she was taking Mrs. Edmonds' place for a while, so that their hostess could see some of the other exhibits.

It was clear that she wasn't about to take off for the Blackfoot reserve or anywhere else, so Don and his father walked over to the old homestead and the corral where Tracy and Tizz were providing atmosphere. They found a group of youngsters massed at the fence, reaching in eager hands. Tracy was proudly leading her pony from one end of the fence to the other, to give all of them a chance for a pat.

Don was sure of her answer before he asked the question, but he asked it, anyhow. "Thank you," Tracy said, "but I couldn't leave Tizz two days in a row."

While they missed having "their women" along, Don liked going alone with his father, as the two drove out to the Indian reserve together. At first, all they could see when they got there were the homes of the Indian superintendent and his assistants, and their office building.

They went into the office, where a helpful Indian agent drew a little map showing the house where Leonard Foxchief lived. Without that map they would never have been able to find it, as it was miles away, in the middle of what seemed like nowhere.

The house was small but well kept up. The first thing Don noticed was the TV antenna on top of it. There was no question that this was Leonard's house, as he was sitting on the step of the low porch. His right leg, bandaged over a splint, was held before him, and he was practicing rope tricks.

If he was surprised to see his visitors, Leonard Foxchief didn't show it as he greeted them with a casual, "Hello." His slow smile lighted his face as he added, "I would ask you to sit down, but where?"

"This looks good enough for me," Don's father said, settling down on the low stoop with Leonard.

Don followed, explaining, "I heard you were hurt, and wanted to find out how you were feeling."

Leonard indicated his ankle. "Only a small fracture — but enough to put me out for the rest of the Stampede."

"You could have stayed in the village, and had fun," Don observed.

Leonard shook his head. "No fun if I can't ride. Here, at least I can be of some use to Grandfather by — like you say — holding down the fort."

Mr. Hill's experienced eyes took in the acreage around the house. "You've got quite a spread here."

Leonard smiled again, that smile that seemed to come from a distance. "Back in 1877 when our band signed its treaty with the government, it

was thought we had made a poor bargain. Most of the best hunting and fishing reserves were already gone. But then with the years the hunting and fishing went too. Our 'poor land' was put to farming and horse-raising, and look at it now."

Mr. Hill looked, and whistled. "Wouldn't mind having this, in Arizona."

Leonard shrugged. "In Arizona maybe you could keep the profits for yourself. Here, all our monies go into the funds of the band. We are, like you say, one great big happy family."

Don looked over the vast stretch of land and asked, "Where do you go to school?"

"This fall, I will go to a regular school in the village. Before, I went to the mission boarding school, like many Indian children do when the big snows come."

Then Leonard grew silent, and began tossing his lariat into the air again. Don couldn't think of anything to say.

His father stood up, asking, "Is there anything we can do for you—get for you?"

"No, thank you. All I need do is to heal."

Don and his father said good-bye, and left. It was miles before they passed a marker indicating the end of the Foxchief land. Don joked, "You certainly couldn't call Leonard 'Lo, the Poor Indian,' could you?"

Mr. Hill answered thoughtfully. "The Foxchief family is an exceptional one, with a lot of drive and ambition. Their band here on the reserve is an exceptional one, too . . . It's funny, though, how the future of generations can depend on luck."

"How do you mean, Dad?"

"Well, how could Leonard's forefathers have guessed that modern farming methods could make what seemed like poor land, rich? Or that in some cases, oil and natural gas would be found in it that could mean a good deal of income for the band?"

"You know what? These Indians are better off than I thought!"

"Only some, Don, only some. The majority can't make a living off their land, and they have a tough time making a go of it."

His father became quiet, thinking about it. Don thought about it, too. But when they got back to the fairgrounds he ran to the infield enclosure to look for Randy. With some of the luck his father had talked about, he might be able to get into the bleachers for the afternoon rodeo!

WAIT TILL YOU'RE READY

Tracy and Sheila, in the corral with Tizz and Pepper, were used to visitors, but they were surprised to find that this time their visitor was Mr. Edmonds. Usually, he was busy elsewhere.

"I've got such good news that it wouldn't keep," he told them. "When we went to the evening show the other night, remember how the grand marshal and the beauty queens on horseback were introduced over the loudspeaker?"

The girls nodded eagerly.

"Well, I've been asked to be an honorary marshal tomorrow night. But wait a minute!" he hurried on as they started to make pleased comments, "that's not the best part of the news. I've been invited to bring you girls along, with Tizz and Pepper, because you've been such a great hit here at Flare Square."

"Ally-oop!" Sheila cried. It was an expression she used which didn't mean much, but it *was* expressive.

Tracy took the news as a personal compliment to her pony. "Won't that be fun, Tizz?" she asked, combing a snarled bit of mane with her fingers.

Looking at Tizz, Mr. Edmonds warned, "We'll have to stand still quite awhile during the chuck-wagon races. Will your pony be able to take it?"

"Of course!" Tracy answered for Tizz. Why, Tizz could do anything she was asked to do! Usually.

"Wait till I tell Randy!" Sheila cried.

"I can't wait to tell Don!" Tracy said.

But they were going to have to wait. Randy and Don were in the infield enclosure at the Stampede, having a bit of excitement of their own.

This was the day Randy was to compete in the boys' steer-riding event. "Time to get lined up," he said in a voice that was carefully calm. He began to saunter over towards the chutes. Don followed him, his own pulse beginning to beat fast.

The man in charge of the event was checking off the names as the contestants showed up. "Randy Edmonds," he checked out loud. Then he added to no one in particular, "We never seem to come out even. First we had more kids signed up than we could use. Today it looks like we're one rider short, on account of Leonard Foxchief dropping out."

Don blinked. This seemed like an answer to

his dreams. Quickly, before he could think it over, he said, "I'd like to ride in Leonard's place."

Randy's head turned sharply. "Think you can, Don?"

Those were fighting words. "Sure I can."

The checker thought it over and said, "It's okay with me if it's okay with your folks."

There was no time to check with his folks. Don spoke in a voice ringing with sureness. "I ride all the time, back in Arizona." He didn't add that so far, he had only ridden horses.

So Don's name was written above Leonard Foxchief's, and he was given a chute number.

The boys who rode out ahead of Don weren't much older or bigger. One was just about his size. He should be able to stick out the time on a steer, Don told himself. If only the palms of his hands would dry up. How could he hang on if his hands were wet?

It was Randy's turn. He drew a lively young steer that was pretty stubborn about having anyone on its back. Randy came out of the chute with a swoosh. No matter how he might feel inside, he did not look frightened a bit.

To Don it seemed that the steer was made of

separate parts rather loosely put together, all of which seemed to be going in different directions. He couldn't figure out how Randy managed to hang on, but Randy did. When the whistle blew as the signal that his time was up, there was a great burst of applause from the grandstand.

Don hoped he could do half as well, now that it was almost his turn. His moist hands were joined by equally unpleasant company. There was a pulse beating hard in his forehead, and his throat felt as if it had been jammed with cotton. But he had wanted to ride a steer since his first day at the Stampede. He had signed up to ride one. The time was now.

The checker was just about to call out his name when Don felt a hand on his shoulder as a voice said, "Scratch this kid's name off the list — he's not ready for steer-riding."

"Okay, Malcolm," the checker said, drawing a line through *Don Hill*. "If you say he's not ready, he's not." Instead, through the loudspeaker, he announced the next name on the list.

Don turned loose his tight feelings on Malcolm. "You don't have any right to say what I can or can't do!"

"Yes, I do," Malcolm said. "You're our guest at the Stampede, and that means we're responsible for you. Getting a broken arm or leg isn't something included in your entertainment."

"Randy made a great ride, didn't he?"

Malcolm drew Don away from the chutes, where everyone couldn't hear them. "Yes, Randy made a great ride, and I'm sure glad he did. Luck was riding with him, but he had more than luck. He had a lot of steer-riding experience that you don't have. You could be thrown hard and really hurt. It's not worth it, Don."

"I guess not." Don spoke slowly, as if he was sorry to have to admit it. It felt pretty good, though, not to have those wet palms, or that pulse beating hard in his forehead, or that stuffed-up feeling in his throat. He wasn't exactly glad Malcolm had stopped him — but he wasn't mad, either.

Malcolm didn't say anything about Don's almost-ride on the way back to the ranch that night, and Don let it pass, too. Everybody was busy talking about what a good show Randy had made. Randy only said modestly, "Heck, luck was riding with me."

At the ranch, Tracy said something she had been trying to say since Sheila had taken such good care of Tizz. "Sheila, would you like to have me sleep in your room tonight?"

"Sure, if you'd like," the little tomboy said in the offhand way she had.

Sheila's room was one of the prettiest Tracy had ever seen. It had two old-fashioned beds with canopies covered with ruffled flowered chintz. Window draperies matched the canopies.

Another surprise was a wall cabinet full of china miniatures. There were many horses, but there were also dogs and cats, and even tiny cups and saucers.

"My grandmother started it for me," Sheila said in her not-that-it-matters kind of a voice when she saw Tracy looking it over. "I keep it up because the winters are pretty long here. The boys won't take me curling with them because I'm still too young."

As she was speaking, Sheila reached up for something, which she handed to Tracy. "When I knew you were coming with Tizz, I got this."

Tracy looked at the miniature in her hand. It was a little Palomino pony like Tizz.

"You can take it with you when you leave, if you like," Sheila went on. "As you can see, it doesn't fit in with my things at all."

In spite of the clumsy way she was putting it, Tracy knew that Sheila was telling her she had really bought the pony for her as a gift. She knew something else, too. Looking at the extra bed with a horse book on the table beside it, and a chair carefully placed close by, she could tell Sheila had planned for her to share the room from the start.

"I'm sorry I didn't come when you first asked me," Tracy said.

"Well, you're here now, so what's the diff?"

Sheila was undressing quickly as she spoke. She got into bed and said, "Good night, Tracy." There was a new ring of warmth in her voice.

"Good night, Sheila." Tracy's voice sounded warm too. She felt warm inside, and *good*.

She was sharing more than a room.

CAN TIZZ TAKE IT?

This was the night!

Tracy, wearing her best western outfit, marched into the infield enclosure on a beautifully groomed Tizz. Sheila, in a fringed jacket and buff-colored slacks, was on her handsome Pepper. Between them, Mr. Edmonds looked impressive, mounted on his beautiful thoroughbred.

When the trio, led by the grand marshal of the Stampede, reached the center of the infield, there was a roll of drums. A voice on the loud-speaker blared out:

"La-a-a-dies and gentlemen! Tonight we have as special guests of honor our good friend, Mr. Keith Edmonds. With him are his daughter Sheila, and a young lady who has come to the Stampede all the way from Tucson, Arizona—Miss Tracy Hill. You've seen Sheila and Tracy in pioneer costume at the old homestead in Flare Square all week. Tonight, you have a chance to see them on dress parade. Let's give the little ladies a hand!"

There was a roar of applause, so loud and sudden that it caused Tizz to prance a bit sidewise. As Mr. Edmonds looked her way with brief

concern, Tracy remembered what he had said about having to stand still for a long time. Could the pony take it? Quickly, Tracy's hand went to Tizz's neck, to pat it soothingly.

Had Tracy allowed herself to think of all those thousands of people in the grandstand, she might have wanted to prance a bit herself. But she pictured only her parents sitting up there. She didn't have to picture Don, because she could see him if she looked.

Don and Randy were in the infield bleachers where they thought it more fun. In fact, they were so close that the girls could hear their teasing

comments, but they pretended not to hear. Instead, they sat erect in their saddles, wrapped in dignity that matched Mr. Edmonds' and the grand marshal's, as they waited for the chuckwagon races to begin.

Right on the dot, the wagons and outriders for the first event entered the infield. They stopped close to where Tracy and Tizz, with the others, stood at attention. Only a fence separated them. Somehow, Tracy hadn't realized she'd be that close.

When the signal to start came, it was as if the cork popped out of a bottle of soda. There was sudden action in all directions. The outriders tossed in the cookstoves and the tent poles, only seconds later the drivers made the figure eights around the barrels with the wagons, and only seconds after that, the outriders leaped onto their horses and galloped after the wagons.

Tizz had never seen so many things happen so swiftly. She blinked in puzzlement. Tracy couldn't see the blink, but she could feel her tremble beneath her. Again, the pony calmed down when she felt Tracy's soothing pat, and remained still.

All of the races were run at a fast pace. Soon it was time for the chuckwagon which the Edmonds ranch sponsored, to compete. Mr. Edmonds had the pleasure of seeing his outfit come in first tonight. This time, Malcolm as an outrider caught up with the wagon in good time, which certainly was an added pleasure. As honorary marshal, though, Mr. Edmonds had to keep his dignity, so the girls did, too. Don and Randy in the bleachers made up for them. The girls could hear their shrill cheers after the others had died down.

It hardly seemed possible that the time had gone so quickly, but already the last race of the evening was about to begin. At the signal, again there was that lightning-swift ritual before the

wagons could hit the track.

This time two of the wagons made the figure eight around their barrels at exactly the same time, as if in a drill. One of the wagons swayed a bit to the outside, just enough for a wheel to catch onto the wheel of the wagon circling the barrels next to it.

There was a sickening clunk, and a wheel of the outside wagon came off. The wagon teetered, then fell against the fence of the enclosure where the grand marshal and the honorary marshals for the evening were standing. The driver leaped out, unhurt, and attendants brought the four horses to a stop before they could get out into the ring.

But the noise and confusion were upsetting to those inside the small enclosure. For a moment, it appeared as if that toppling wagon was going to land upon them, in spite of that fence.

Mr. Edmonds knew it wouldn't, and he held his ground firmly, as did the grand marshal. Tizz gave a nervous sidestep, and tried to pull away from that fence against which the wagon had overturned. But Tracy kept her head, and held Tizz's firmly. She forgot her own fear and remembered only Mr. Edmonds' concern about whether Tizz could take it, as she spoke soothingly to her pony. The calm words and her prompt action took effect. Tizz stayed where she was. Her sides heaved a bit, but she held her ground.

It was with surprise that Tracy realized she and Tizz stood alone with Mr. Edmonds. The high-bred and high-spirited Pepper was racing around the enclosure. A startled and annoyed Sheila strained at the reins and dug in her heels until she brought the gelding to a stop, and trotted him back to his place.

"Are you all right, Sheila?" Mr. Edmonds asked. He was asking it of *Sheila*, Tracy thought in wonder.

"I'm all right," Sheila answered shortly, "but I don't know what got into Pepper."

When the chuckwagon races were over, the grand marshal and the honorary marshals paraded out of the infield enclosure. The thunder of applause followed after them. If Sheila had been cross about Pepper's behavior, she forgot it at the sound of that applause.

Tonight when the Edmonds' and the Hills were driving back to the ranch, something new had been added. A trailer which carried Tizz and Pepper. Since it was so close to the end of the Hills' stay at the ranch, it was thought best that Tizz should have a day of freedom before starting on another journey. If Tracy was not going to appear at Flare Square, Sheila did not want to appear alone, so Pepper was going home, too.

The talk in the station wagon centered around

the excitement of the falling chuckwagon. "Well," Mr. Edmonds said, "Tizz certainly proved she could take it. So did you, Tracy. If you had panicked, Tizz might have."

"I didn't panic," Sheila put in quickly. "Only Pepper did." She spoke lightly, her earlier annoyance gone. When they got to the ranch she said, "You'll spend the night with me, won't you, Tracy?"

"Of course."

In the room, Tracy hesitated before turning out the light. Finally she said slowly, "I'm used to saying good night to Tizz before I get into bed, when she's near."

"Well, go ahead," Sheila said. "She's right out there in the guest corral. Pepper's 'way off in the big corral, and it would take forever to find him."

Tracy put on her jacket over her pajamas and slipped outdoors. A steady wind was blowing across the Alberta plains. Although it was late, the great bowl of sky still had patches of light here and there, between the stars.

Tizz looked tiny in the corral, smaller than she had seemed before. Tracy realized this was because there were such great spaces all around.

The ranchland spread out, flat or gently rolling,
in all directions as far as she could see.

Tracy too felt smaller than she had felt inside

the house. Feeling small like this gave her a funny feeling. As she fondled Tizz, she murmured, "Canada's a long way from home, Tizz. Are you lonesome?"

Tracy's hand was caught in a strand of her pony's mane. To free it, Tizz shook her head sidewise.

But Tracy thought she was saying no. "You're right," she said, putting both arms around Tizz's neck. Why, how could either one get lonesome when they were together?